THE OTHER SIDE OF MAGIC

STARSCAPE BOOKS BY
DEBBIE DADEY
AND MARCIA THORNTON JONES

THE
OTHER SIDE
OF
MAGIC

Debbie Dadey and Marcia Thornton Jones

Illustrated by Adam Stower

A TOM DOHERTY ASSOCIATES BOOK • NEW YORK

This is a work of fiction. All the characters, organizations, and events portrayed in this novel are either products of the authors' imaginations or are used fictitiously.

KEYHOLDERS #2: THE OTHER SIDE OF MAGIC

Copyright © 2009 Debra S. Dadey and Marcia Thornton Jones

Inside the Magic excerpt copyright © 2009 by Debra S. Dadey and Marcia Thornton Jones

Illustrations and maps copyright © 2009 by Adam Stower

A Starscape Book
Published by Tom Doherty Associates, LLC
175 Fifth Avenue
New York, NY 10010

www.tor-forge.com

ISBN 978-0-7653-5983-4

First Edition: May 2009

Printed in the United States of America by Offset Paperback Manufacturers, Dallas, Pennsylvania.

0   9   8   7   6   5   4   3

To my wonderful family,
you are the keys to my happiness.
—DD

To Steve Jones, a Keyholder to all that's important,
and to my links Calliope and CocoMo!
—MTJ

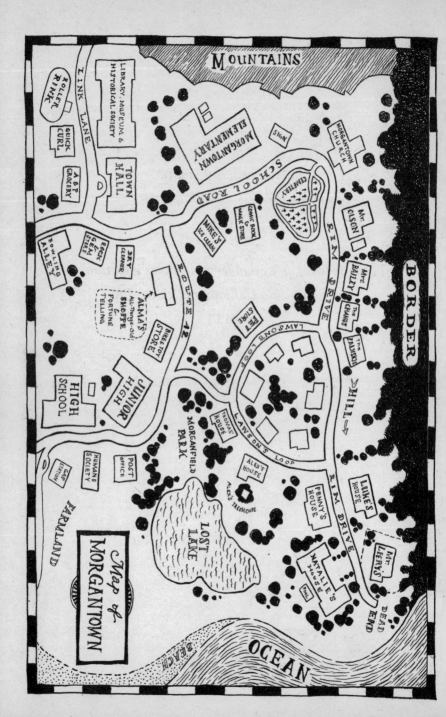

1

"Can she breathe? Quick! Somebody do CPR!" Buttercup the rat cried, putting her paws on her cheeks in rat panic. She gnawed on Natalie's shoelaces.

Natalie sat in a kitchen chair in the middle of Mr. Leery's kitchen. Her mouth opened and closed like a guppy, but no sounds came out. A pink notebook slipped from her lap and smacked onto the floor, startling the rat on her sneakers.

Penny and Luke stared at Natalie. They had never gotten along with their neighbor and fifth-grade classmate, mostly because she always bragged about everything her dad bought her. But that didn't mean they liked seeing Natalie gasping for breath.

"Well, this is going well," Mo said sarcastically. Mr. Leery's black cat sat on top of the counter. He lifted a huge paw and casually cleaned the tuft of hair between his ears.

"Hush, Mo," Mr. Leery said. "The girl has suffered a shock. Give her time to get used to the idea. I'm sure she'll be fine."

"Natalie Lawson has never been fine," Luke muttered. "And she's never been speechless, either."

Penny swatted Luke on the arm. "Well, there's a first time for everything," she said. "Now, be nice."

"Why?" Luke asked. "It's Natalie. She's never nice to us."

"Oh dear, oh dear," Mr. Leery said, bending down in front of Natalie and snapping his fingers in front of her eyes. "Talk to me, child."

Natalie's eyes slowly focused on the old man. For as long as anyone could remember, Mr. Leery had lived in this small cottage at the dead end of the last street in Morgantown. Everyone thought he was harmless. Luke and Penny knew he was much more than that, and now Natalie was beginning to find out how deceiving looks could be.

"Rats," Natalie mumbled as she gradually remembered where she was. "I saw rats. Here. Your house. It's infested. With rats. Must tell. My father."

"No, no, no," Luke said. "Don't you remember a word of what we told you?"

Penny and Luke had helped Mr. Leery explain everything to Natalie. But as soon as she'd seen the dragon and unicorn she'd totally blanked out.

"This isn't a rat," Penny said, pointing to the animal perched on Natalie's shoe.

"Yes, it is," Mo purred. "A big, fat, juicy one."

Buttercup squeaked and gnawed on the lace edge of Natalie's sock.

"Shh, Mo," Mr. Leery said. "You're not helping."

Penny started over. "Okay. This *is* a rat. But it's not a normal everyday kind of rat. She's your link. Just like Kirin is my link."

At the sound of her name, a unicorn clomped into the kitchen from the living room to gaze at Natalie. "How many times do we have to go over this?" the unicorn snapped. "I'm hungry."

"And Dracula is my link," Luke added, ignoring Kirin's complaint.

"That's me! That's me!" sang a dragon the size of a Doberman pinscher as he flapped into the kitchen. The kitchen was too small for his wings and he ruffled everyone's hair as he searched for a place to land.

"They came from the other side of the border," Penny explained.

Everyone in Morgantown knew about the thorny bushes at the edge of their town that had been there for as long as they could remember. What they didn't realize was that the bushes formed a magical border between what was real and what was magic. The only people who were allowed to know were the Keyholders, a force of three whose job it was to maintain the border.

"Mr. Leery chose us as the new Keyholders," Luke said. "It's going to be our job to make sure magic stays out of our world."

"To be a Keyholder you have to be chosen by a link from the other side of magic," Mr. Leery added. "And this very special creature chose you."

Natalie glanced down at Buttercup. The rat stopped gnawing long enough to give Natalie a small wave with her paw. The color disappeared from Natalie's face and she shuddered. She looked up. Her eyes landed on the unicorn peering over Penny's shoulder.

"Back up," Penny told the unicorn. "Give Natalie some room to breathe."

When Kirin took a step backward, she trampled Dracula's tail. Dracula swooped up, knocking over a pitcher of water on the counter. Buttercup squeaked as the pitcher smashed to the floor within inches of her tail. Kirin auto-matically tossed her head at the high-pitched sound, her horn catching in the curtains and ripping them off the window.

"Enough!" Mr. Leery bellowed and raised his arms. The room fell silent.

Except for Natalie. Natalie whimpered.

"I would not have placed this burden on you at this time if it wasn't an emergency," Mr. Leery said. "But it is. Two Keyholders are gone and I can no longer protect the border by myself. My magic is not strong enough alone. Already the border is weakening. I need your help, Natalie. Yours and Penny's and Luke's. Unfortunately, we'll have to wait to have your official ceremony. For now, I will give you this for . . . protection." Mr. Leery pulled the bracelet from his wrist. It was silver like Penny's and Luke's, but this one had a purple stone. It was a perfect match to the collar dangling from Buttercup's neck, the very one that used to hang on Mo.

"That silver will keep the boggarts and goblins away," Kirin said with a nod of her horn. "That and bells work every time."

Dracula flapped his wings so that he could hop up and down. "Bells! Bells! I like bells!"

"But I don't want to be what you said," Natalie whispered. "A Keyholder."

"Too late," Luke said. "You already are one. The rat picked you."

Buttercup spit out a shoelace. "Just barely in time. I say, *barely* in time," she babbled. "Because the Queen of the Boggarts is out to get us, one and all!"

2

Natalie blinked as if she were waking up from a nightmare. Then she looked at Mr. Leery. "Why does Penny have a unicorn for a link and Luke gets a dragon? And why do I have an r-a-t?" She spelled the word so she wouldn't have to say it.

"Because that is the link who chose you," Mr. Leery said patiently.

"But it's not fair!" Natalie wailed. "I'm going to tell my father!"

"No!" everyone shouted at once. Everyone except Dracula. The dragon burped, sending a tendril of flame across the counter. A kitchen towel shot up in flames.

"Oh, bother," Kirin said and slapped her silky tail over the flames to smother them.

When Mr. Leery kneeled in front of Natalie, the rat scooted under the table. Mr. Leery held Natalie's hands in his own. "You cannot tell anyone," Mr. Leery said. "The life of a Keyholder is one of secrecy. It's the way it must be."

"Besides, your dad would think you're crazy," Penny told her.

"Maybe I am," Natalie said. "I think you're making this whole thing up. I bet this unicorn is some sort of costume and the dragon is a big robot. This is just a practical joke you're playing on me. You've never liked me and now you're trying to embarrass me. If you think I'm falling for this, you can think again. Where's the camera? You better not be planning on plastering this on the Internet. You'll be *sorry* because I'll tell my father, and he's a judge."

Natalie pulled her hands away from Mr. Leery and jumped up so fast Mr. Leery sat back on the floor. She pushed past Penny, grabbed Kirin's horn and pulled. Hard. "This is a costume. Right?"

The moment Natalie touched Kirin, the unicorn tossed her head back. "That's plain rude," Kirin said. "Nobody touches a unicorn, except of course, a link."

"Very funny," Natalie said. "Who's under that costume? Is that your sister, Luke? And some of her friends?"

"Kirin is real," Penny said. "Just like Dracula."

"What kind of name is Dracula for a dragon?" Natalie snapped.

Kirin defended her friend. "Dracula is a very old and powerful name. Just because some humdrums tried to ruin it doesn't mean it's bad."

"What's that word? *Humdrum*. What are you talking about?" Natalie demanded with a stomp of her foot.

"You," Kirin said simply.

"How dare you call me names? Wait until my father finds out. That's considered bullying, you know," Natalie fumed.

"No, no, no," Mr. Leery said, pulling himself up from the floor. "Humdrums are what people from this side of the border are called."

"You know. Regular people," Luke added.

"Kirin and Dracula are from the other side. They're magical," Penny added.

Natalie glared at Dracula. "I don't believe a word you're saying. Aren't dragons supposed to be bigger?"

Dracula bounced up and down on the kitchen counter. The wooden cabinets groaned under his weight. His head tapped the ceiling with every bounce, leaving a dark spot on the paint. "Bigger soon. I get bigger. Eat more turkberries."

"No!" Luke told him. "No more turkberries. You know they make you sneeze."

"He can't be real," Natalie said. "I bet it's some kind of robot. Is this your science project or something?" Natalie took three giant steps across the kitchen to pull on Dracula's red nose.

"Ouch!" Dracula bellowed. "What's the big idea? I need that nose. How else can I breathe fire?"

"Breathe fire?" Natalie squeaked, beginning to feel dizzy from all the magic.

"Of course," said Dracula. "I've got the best fire breath for a dragon my age. Want to see? Look! I'll show you!"

"No!" shouted Luke. "We don't want to burn down Mr. Leery's house."

Natalie looked from Dracula to Luke to Kirin to Penny to the black cat named Mo. "What about the cat?" Natalie asked.

"Hands off," Mo warned. "I'm with Leery."

"You talk!" Natalie said. "I knew it!"

"Mo is a very special . . . cat," Mr. Leery told Natalie.

"Then it's real?" Natalie asked the links. "You're all real?"

"As real as the math test on Friday," Luke told her.

Natalie stumbled back to the chair and sat down with a giant oomph. As soon as she did, Buttercup scurried out from under the table and gnawed on Natalie's already frayed shoelace.

Natalie looked down at the rat on her sneakers. Then she looked up hopefully at Kirin. "Couldn't we trade?" Natalie begged. "I'd be a much better link for a unicorn than Penny. I have a huge room over my garage where you could sleep. Whatever you like to eat, I can get it for you. I'm so rich, I could build you your own stable. Or even a castle."

"Stop trying to steal my unicorn," Penny

snapped. She knew she sounded mean, but just the thought of losing Kirin felt like someone punching her in the stomach.

"Don't worry about her," Kirin said. She didn't even look at Natalie. Instead, the unicorn turned her head toward Penny. Penny could see a small reflection of herself in Kirin's liquid blue eyes. "A unicorn is faithful," Kirin said. "I will always be your link. Always."

"Well," said Natalie, turning to look at the red-nosed dragon. "Then I'll take the dragon."

"Take me? Take me?" Dracula screeched. "Take me where? Where is she taking me, Luke? Are you going, too?"

"Shh," Luke said, smoothing down the scales on Dracula's nose. "We're not going anywhere. Calm down before you explode."

Dracula exploding was a very real possibility. Two wisps of smoke curled from the dragon's nostrils. Everyone in the room held their breaths as Luke calmly rubbed the dragon's nose until the smoke disappeared.

Mr. Leery cleared his throat. "Natalie, once a link has chosen you, it cannot be undone. It is for always."

Mo jumped off the counter onto Mr. Leery's shoulder, and curled around the old man's neck. "Forever," Mo repeated with a purr.

"Or at least for two hundred years, because that's how long each trio of Keyholders is in charge," Penny said.

"Oh dear, oh dear," Mr. Leery said. "Not in charge. Not yet. You're simply not ready. You need training. You and your links."

At his words, Penny placed her hand on Kirin's neck. Luke automatically moved next to Dracula. It was almost as if a magnet pulled them close together.

Natalie stomped her foot, totally forgetting about the rat clinging to her laces. Buttercup flew across the room, her whiskers trembling.

"You mean I'll be stuck with a rat for the rest of my life?" Natalie yelled.

"Shh," Penny told Natalie. "You'll hurt Buttercup's feelings."

"Rats don't have feelings!" Natalie screeched.

"Are you sure about that?" Luke asked, pointing to the floor.

Buttercup picked up her tail and walked out of the kitchen without saying a word.

Mr. Leery put his hands together and looked sharply at Natalie. "Things are not always what they seem. The sooner you realize that, the happier you will be."

"I'd be happier with a better link. Couldn't I have a fairy or a mermaid?" Natalie asked.

"How about a giant troll with yellow teeth and green hair?" Luke said with a grin. For once, he thought, Natalie got exactly what she deserved. A rat.

Mo arched his back and hissed at Natalie. "The day will come when you thank your lucky stars that you have Buttercup, for she is worth a thousand fairies, a million mermaids, and hundreds of ogres. Just wait and see!"

Natalie looked into the living room at Buttercup. She was just a rat, wasn't she?

3

At school the next day, Natalie definitely didn't look like the prissy girl everyone was used to. Her hair stuck up in knots and nothing she wore matched. That wasn't the worst thing. Her clothes actually had tiny holes all over them, even her shoes. She slowly walked up the sidewalk as if she were sleepwalking. She clutched her pink notebook over her chest like a shield. The eight-armed rubber ogre on top of her pencil trembled with every step she took.

No one could believe that Natalie, the richest

and most spoiled girl in Morgantown, had holes in her clothes.

Penny and Luke waited until the other kids had gone into school before pulling Natalie behind the Morgantown Elementary sign. "What happened to you?" Penny asked when she was sure they were alone.

"Are teeny tiny holes a new fashion trend?" Luke teased.

Natalie looked at Penny and Luke as though they were strangers, but finally she shuddered and started talking. "Nightmares," she said. "I had nightmares. All night long."

"Nightmares are bad," Penny said.

When Natalie spoke her voice shook. "These were worse than bad. They were terrible, awful, horrible nightmares."

"What did you dream about?" Luke asked.

"Trolls," Natalie said. "Hairy trolls and ogres covered in warts."

Luke laughed. "That's what you get for having that silly pencil topper you're always waving under people's noses," he told her.

Natalie had started carrying around her pink notebook and pencil during the summer. She took it everywhere she went so she could write down what people did. She called herself a spy. Other people called her nosy. And that was just the nice people. Some called her worse.

Natalie held up her pencil and shook her head. "This isn't the kind of ogre that was in my dreams," she said. "I dreamed about the real kind. The kind that live on *the other side of magic.*" She whispered the last part even though no one was within hearing distance.

Luke and Penny glanced over their shoulders. They weren't watching for other kids. They were looking for shadows that might've crept over the border that separated their world from the land of magic. Before they left Mr. Leery's cottage the night before, Mr. Leery had warned them that the Queen of Boggarts would be determined to halt the transfer of Keyholder powers from Mr. Leery to them. Once she did that, she could destroy the border between the magic and real world. Then every evil creature could easily invade the world that they had always known as real.

"You don't really think they'd come here for us, do you?" Natalie asked.

Penny gripped Natalie by the shoulders and looked straight into her eyes. "The Queen already sent a boggart spy. Remember Bobby? He was one of *them*. And he came right into our classroom."

Bobby was a spy sent by the Queen of Boggarts to find out who Mr. Leery had selected to apprentice as Keyholders. Penny and Luke found out the hard way that boggarts were skillful shape-shifters. When they had seen what a real boggart was like, they found out fast that not all creatures from the other side of magic were wonderful like Kirin, Dracula, and Mo.

The skies around the school were oppressively cloudy. A gray fog stretched across the playground. "Those ugly boggart spies could be watching us right now," Luke warned, as he looked around. "No place is safe when it comes to boggarts."

"What if she sends more spies . . . or something even worse to try to stop us from learning to be Keyholders?" Penny asked.

"What could be worse than boggarts?" Natalie asked.

Luke pointed to the rubber eraser on the tip of Natalie's pencil. "Ogres, for one thing," he pointed out.

Penny shuddered as she thought of more possibilities. She had started reading some of Mr. Leery's books about magical creatures. Many of the beasts' pictures were so horrifying she'd had to skip over some pages.

"We'll worry about boggarts and ogres when we have to. Right now we need to find out what happened to Natalie's clothes." Penny said. She turned to Natalie. "Tell us."

Natalie's lip trembled and she sniffed. "It's Buttercup's fault. She nibbles when she's nervous."

"Buttercup?" Luke blurted. "You actually have a nervous rat?"

Natalie wailed, "Why do I have to have an r-a-t!" Natalie still couldn't bring herself to say the word out loud. She looked at Luke and Penny. Her eyes went from teary to plain old mad.

"It's not fair that I have a you-know-what," she said. "ME! Who would've thought that Natalie Lawson would end up with an r-a-t?" And then she marched off.

Luke looked at Penny. "It's really not that surprising."

"Shh," Penny warned him, but she couldn't help laughing.

Later that day, Penny and Luke found little to laugh about.

Penny got in trouble for rolling her eyes and being sarcastic to the teacher during math, and when Natalie was caught chewing on the corner of her spelling test Luke laughed so hard he got a really bad case of the hiccups. They got louder and louder with each hiccup. The rest of the class giggled with every hiccup.

"Enough!" Mr. Crandle bellowed. He glared at Penny, Natalie, and Luke. "Out," he said. "Maybe sitting in the principal's office will cure you three of your shenanigans."

"What is happening to us?" Natalie whined as the three sat in the principal's office. She chewed on a piece of her hair and looked around. "My father is not going to like it that I was sent to the office."

"Well, eating a hole in your spelling test wasn't the smartest thing in the world to do," Penny snorted.

Luke looked at his friend and hiccupped.

Natalie spit out the strand of hair. "Are you

calling me stupid?" she asked. Then she started gnawing on her ogre eraser.

"Well, duh. You're not exactly the sharpest pencil in the teacher's desk," Penny snapped.

That made Luke hiccup again.

"I'm in trouble and you're making jokes. This is no time for sarcasm," Natalie told her. "Monsters from the other side could be hunting us down as we speak, and what's worse, I've been sent to the principal's office! You sound as bad as Luke's sister and all her teenage friends."

"No, she doesn't," Luke said. "She sounds worse. She sounds like her link!"

And then Luke hiccupped again.

4

"I want answers, and I want them now," Natalie said after school. "Mr. Leery has a whole lot more explaining to do."

Penny agreed. Luke just hiccupped and headed down the sidewalk toward Mr. Leery's house. Natalie and Penny followed. But the kids didn't get far. As they turned the corner onto Rim Drive, the street they lived on, they heard a limb crack overhead.

Penny looked up and screamed. Three ugly beasts stared down at them. They were small, monkey-like creatures with pointed ears, yellow eyes, and slobber dripping from their snarling mouths. A huge blob fell from the biggest creature's mouth and splatted right on Natalie's head.

Plop! The goo on Natalie's head brought high-pitched giggles from the beasts.

"I did it," bragged one of the creatures.

"No, me did it," said another.

"No, no, no. Me. Me. Me," said the third. The three creatures pushed each other back and forth on the creaking branch, with slobber dribbling down their chests.

"Yuck!" Natalie screeched, trying to wipe slimy goo from her head.

Penny and Luke did what any self-respecting kid would do. They ran. In fact, they ran half a block before they realized Natalie wasn't with them.

"Stop," Penny said, grabbing Luke's arm. "We have to go back for her."

"No, we don't," Luke told her. "Natalie wouldn't come back for us."

"Do you want to be like Natalie?" Penny asked.

Luke glared at Penny. Then he hiccupped. "Fine. We'll go back."

The two friends crept back until they spotted Natalie in the middle of the sidewalk slinging slobber off her head. But this was not normal slobber. This was bright green and slimy. It clung to Natalie's hands and hung from her hair in long glistening strands. "This is so gross. I'm telling my father," Natalie complained.

What Natalie didn't know was that the slobber she was flinging off her head was striking the creatures, keeping them from getting her.

"You hit me," one beast yelled as green slime smacked his eyes. He slung the goop back over his head, hitting the second beast on the nose.

"Ouch!" yelled the second monster. It fell back into the third creature, who pushed him back.

"Get off! Get off!" screeched the third beast,

as he tried to knock the second, rather plump, creature off his foot.

The chubby monster slipped and fell all the way to the ground. When he jumped up, he ran smack-dab into the tree. The branches above him swayed and the other two beasts teetered on the edge of the limbs.

"Natalie!" Luke yelled. "Come on!"

But Natalie was too worried about her hair to pay any attention to Luke.

"We have to go help her," Penny said.

"Why?" Luke said. "Maybe the boggarts will take her to LaLa Land and we'll be rid of her." Natalie had bugged him for as long as he could remember. She never missed a chance to irritate him.

"That is exactly what the Queen of Boggarts would like," Penny said. "Because then the Keyholders' force would be broken and she could slip right into our world and take over. But look closer. They aren't boggarts. These creatures are even worse."

It took all the courage he could muster, but Luke wasn't about to let Penny know he was scared. He ran beside the monsters and grabbed Natalie's arms. Together, he and Penny pulled Natalie down the street.

Of course, it's almost impossible to outrun a magical creature, and truly impossible to outrun three, especially when they can jump from tree branch to tree branch. But these were not the most coordinated of monsters. Luckily for the three kids, the creatures' arms and legs got tangled and they fell down in a heap, giving the kids just enough time to escape their grasp.

"Quick!" Luke said. "Get in here." The kids dashed into Mr. Olson's empty garage and slammed the small side door.

Wham!

Wham!

WHAM!

Penny snapped the lock shut just as the three creatures crashed into the door.

Penny and Luke leaned over, trying to catch their breaths. Outside, they heard scratching and snuffling.

"What do we do now?" Luke gasped.

"We get help." Natalie pulled a cell phone from her pocket. She was one of the few kids in their class to have her very own phone, but at this second, Penny and Luke were glad she had one.

"I'm calling my father. Those evil creatures will be run out of town." Natalie punched numbers into her phone. "Hello? Hello?" she yelled. She looked at the blank screen of her phone. "Of all the times for the battery to die. I'm going to make my daddy get me a new one."

"When was the last time you charged your phone?" Luke asked.

"None of your business," Natalie told him as she shoved the phone back in her pocket. "It's impossible to think with all this goo on my head. I can't wait to go to the Quick Curl to get a vanilla-buttermilk shampoo and coconut massage." Natalie groaned and wiped slobber off her forehead.

"We have more to worry about than shampoos right now," Penny told her. "We're trapped!"

"I want my daddy," Natalie whimpered just like a three-year-old.

"You know you can't tell your father about the other side of magic," Luke said as the creatures giggled outside the door. Luke was definitely sure that giggling meant the monsters had come up with an idea. And he was pretty sure he wasn't going to like it one bit.

"We'll see about that," Natalie said. "I tell my father everything. And he is not going to be happy to know that boggarts are terrorizing ME."

"Let's just try to get out of this mess right now," Penny said, thankful that the door had a lock. "Besides, those aren't boggarts. They're goblins."

"How do you know that?" Luke asked.

"From Mr. Leery. He has a shelf full of old books and he let me borrow one. I found out lots of stuff, like boggarts and goblins don't like silver. And they both are servants of the Queen. But there is one good thing about goblins."

"I can't imagine a single good thing about those slime-slinging, ugly monsters," Natalie griped.

"What is it?" Luke asked.

"Goblins are not the smartest creatures," Penny told them. "In fact, they're stupid. That's why the Queen of Boggarts had no trouble enlisting them to do her evil deeds."

"Great," Luke said. "All we have to do is outwit three goofy goblins. That shouldn't be so hard, right? After all, we're smart. Right?"

Natalie flung back her hair, sending tendrils of slime against the grimy window. "At least I am."

"Does everyone have their bracelets on?" Penny asked.

The three kids pulled up their sleeves to reveal the antique bracelets that Mr. Leery had given them for protection.

"I thought this was supposed to keep bad stuff away," Natalie said.

"I thought so, too," Luke said.

"Well, we need new ones because these old ones don't seem to be doing the trick," Natalie said.

Luke looked at Penny. He was worried that for once Natalie might be right. Could the bracelets not have enough magic to protect them?

"Maybe these goblins don't know the rules," Natalie said.

"Or maybe they *are* working. After all, they didn't hurt us," Penny pointed out.

"Excuse me," Natalie said. "I have a pound of slobber in my hair. If that's not hurt then I don't know what is."

"Penny's right," Luke said. "They could have grabbed us and taken us to the other side of magic and straight to the Queen herself. But they didn't. Maybe the bracelets do help."

"What if we run as fast as we can to Mr. Leery's house?" Penny suggested and reached her hand toward the lock.

"Are you nuts?" Natalie said, grabbing Penny's hand. "I'm not going out there without some kind of weapon."

The kids looked around the garage. It was a small, musty-smelling garage that was more like a shed than anything. One wall was lined with old, green-painted wooden shelves. Cans of paint, motor oil, and old cardboard boxes filled the shelves.

"None of this stuff can help us," Natalie complained. "I can't believe I picked today to forget to charge my cell phone."

"What about this?" Luke asked. He patted one of three battered metal trash cans. They were rusty and filled with bulging black plastic garbage bags.

Penny smiled. "They do look like silver! And something silver is just what we need. Maybe they'll fool the goblins. Luke, you're a genius!"

When Luke and Penny explained the plan to Natalie, she immediately threw up her hands in protest. "No way!"

Penny put her hands on her hips. "Do you want to stay in here until that goblin goo dries on your head?"

"Who knows?" Luke said with a grin. "That stuff might never come out once it dries. Your hair may turn slobber-color forever."

Natalie's eyes got wide and her hands flew to her slimy hair. "All right, but if anyone from school ever hears about this, my life will be over."

"Your life may very well be over if we don't escape those goblins," Penny pointed out while

Luke emptied each garbage can onto the floor.

A putrid smell wafted up from the plastic bags and Natalie put her hands over her mouth. "I think I'm going to be sick."

Penny had to admit that the stench was pretty bad, but the screech of the goblins outside the door was worse, so she did what she had to do. She pulled the stinky trash can over her head, leaving just her legs sticking out.

"All right," Luke told the girls. "As soon as I push the garage door opener, start running toward Mr. Leery's house as fast as you can."

"How am I supposed to do that?" Natalie asked. "I won't be able to see a thing with this stupid trash can over my head."

"Just follow the sidewalk toward his house. Look at your feet and you should be okay." Luke put his hand on the garage door opener and got ready to put his trash can on.

Natalie held the can over her head. "I can't

believe I'm doing this. Ewwwww! This is so gross. This is so gross. This is so gross."

Luckily, the trash can muffled Natalie's complaining, and Luke pushed the garage door button. The door-opener whirled and the automatic door lurched up. Luke dropped the can over his head and walked out of the garage with Penny and Natalie following.

Luke was surprised at how easily they got out of the garage, and except for the smell, he did very well. He could see the sidewalk under his feet and he'd walked this way so many times that he could probably do it blindfolded. In his mind, he called off the houses they passed: Mrs. Bailey's, the Changs', next would be the Zaluskis'. Overhead, he heard the gibberish of the goblins as they hopped from branch to branch. Leaves and sticks pinged against the shell of his trash can. It was just down the hill to his house and Mr. Leery's.

"It's working," Penny called from under her

trash can. She wished she had kept quiet, because just then a very loud screech came from overhead.

"Oh, great!" Natalie wailed. "I've got a trash can on my head and those monsters are still going to get me!"

"Keep moving and watch out for the tree root," Luke said. He stepped over the big root that poked up from the sidewalk in front of the Zaluskis' house. Penny hopped over it next.

"This is the worst thing that has ever happened to me," Natalie complained. "This is just not worth it." Natalie was so busy fussing that she didn't hear Luke's warning. She didn't see the tree root until it was too late.

Crash! Natalie fell to the ground and started rolling inside her trash can. Her pink notebook and ogre pencil flew off into the shrubs.

Whack! Natalie rolled into Penny.

Crash! Penny fell to the ground.

Whack! Penny's trash can rolled into Luke's.

If Mrs. Zaluski had looked out the window while changing little Richard's diaper, she would have seen three trash cans rolling down the hill in front of her house. She might have rushed out to help the kids trapped inside. But she didn't, and the kids rolled faster and faster down the hill.

Swinging in the trees above them were three very ugly and very angry goblins.

5

Smack!

Smack!

Smack!

The three kids slammed into Mr. Leery's fence. None of them moved.

A loud roar brought Luke to his senses. It was just outside his trash can. He quickly pulled his feet inside the trash can and waited for the worst, but nothing happened. After a few minutes, something furry grabbed his foot.

Luke shook his leg and yelled, "Let go of me, you ugly goblin!"

"Meownooooooooooo. Do I look like a goblin?" Mo snapped.

Luke scrambled out of the trash can and looked around. Mo sat beside him, licking a paw. A purple feather fluttered by his tail. Luke looked up in the trees, but he only saw the blue sky and a small robin flying by. The goblins had disappeared.

Beside Luke, two battered trash cans lay on their sides. Natalie's legs stuck out of one and Penny's out of the other. Neither pair of legs moved. "Are they okay?" Luke asked.

"I've just rolled down the hill in a stinky trash can," Natalie snapped as she scrambled out of her trash can. "I am covered in goblin goo and stale coffee grounds. How in the world could I possibly be okay?"

Natalie sat on the ground. Her face was splattered with brown smudges and a lettuce leaf sat on her shoulder. Goblin slobber caked the top of her head. "I will never get over this, Luke

Morgan. Never! I can't believe I let you talk me into this."

Luke never paid any attention to Natalie, but he especially didn't just then. "Penny?" he called. "Are you all right?"

Not a sound came from Penny's trash can. Her legs remained still. "Penny!" Luke shouted and crawled over to her. He pulled the trash can off her head. She lay on the damp grass with her eyes closed.

"Penny!" Luke yelled again. Immediately, Mr. Leery was beside him. He gently lifted Penny and took her inside his house.

"We'd better call an ambulance," Natalie said, marching behind Mr. Leery. "She probably hit her head. It's a wonder we weren't all killed. Wait until I tell my father. He's a judge, you know. He'll send whoever is responsible straight to jail." Natalie cast an angry look at Luke as everyone went inside the cottage.

"No need," Mr. Leery said before calling "Kirin!" He laid Penny on his cot and instantly the unicorn pushed open the back door and clattered through the house to stand over Penny.

"I knew it! I could sense something wrong," Kirin said. "I told you we needed to go to school. This is exactly why we should never be separated." Kirin touched Penny's forehead gently with her horn.

Even though Mr. Leery had convinced the giant spider named Snuffles, who lived in the border, to weave a web of invisibility for the links, Mr. Leery refused to let them accompany the kids to school. "The web could slip," he had told them. "Or tear. No, no, no. Best the links stay here with me. At least for the time being."

Penny's eyes fluttered open and she smiled up at her link. "What . . . what happened to the goblins?" Penny stammered. "How did I get here?"

Mo turned and licked the tip of his tail. "I chased them away," he said, as if battling goblins was an everyday occurrence.

Mr. Leery held up his hands to silence everyone. "Did you say goblins?" Mr. Leery asked. "Here? On this side of the border?"

"Three of them," Luke told him. "They ambushed us after school."

Natalie stood in the doorway, looking at Kirin's horn in amazement. "Did he just magically heal Penny?"

Kirin tossed her silky white mane. "I *am* a unicorn, you know."

Natalie held up a broken fingernail. "Could you fix this? I chipped it rolling down the hill."

"Oh dear, oh dear," Mr. Leery said, without glancing at Natalie. "We can't wait any longer. We'll have to get started right away."

"On what?" Penny said, popping up from the cot.

"Your lessons, of course," Mr. Leery said.

"Lessons?" Luke said. He didn't like the sound of that. School was not his favorite thing, and he certainly didn't need any more homework. He already had to study for a math test.

"Your Keyholder lessons, to be exact," Mr. Leery told him.

"Wait just a minute," Penny said. "Things were very weird at school. We want to find out what's going on."

Dracula hopped into the already crowded bedroom and hiccupped. A small puff of smoke flew out of his nose. "Bad day. Bad day," he muttered. "Need more turkberries."

"No turkberries!" Luke told him.

Dracula nuzzled close to Luke. "Bad day. Bad day."

Just then Buttercup scooted into the room between Natalie's legs. Natalie couldn't help but shriek, even though she knew that Buttercup wasn't an ordinary rat.

"No more separations," Buttercup said. "We need to be together."

"No," Luke said. "This day was bad enough. Natalie practically ate her spelling test, Penny was a smart aleck, and the whole class was laughing at me because I kept hiccupping."

Luke stopped talking long enough to realize his hiccups were gone. "Hey, I guess the goblins scared the hiccups out of me."

"Good." Mr. Leery nodded his head. "Very good."

"How is any of that good?" Natalie said. "I had to go to the principal's office. What will my father say?"

Mo laughed. "Meowhahahahahahahahaha."

Penny thought she'd never heard anything so irritating, except the goblins' screeches, of course.

"You've begun to connect with your links," Mr. Leery explained.

"I am not a smart aleck," Kirin said. "I resent that."

Dracula didn't say a word, he just hiccupped.

"You mean like E.S.P.?" Luke asked.

Natalie backed up to the bedroom wall. "I don't want a rat invading my brain," she said.

Mr. Leery shook his head. "It's more of an

emotional bond. Your links were upset to be without you, thus the burping, sarcasm, and gnawing. It's all very new to you, so you don't know how to control it. But never fear; that will be part of your training. And your training starts immediately, before the goblins can accomplish their mission."

"What would they do with us if they caught us?" Natalie asked.

"Believe me," Mo said as he cleaned between two claws. "You do *not* want to know."

Mr. Leery rubbed his bald head. "We cannot let that happen. Goblins are not known for being . . . kind to their captives."

A chill went up Penny's spine and she put her hand on Kirin's back. Kirin turned her head to look at Penny. For just a second, Penny thought she saw tears in Kirin's blue eyes.

6

"We'll have to go over," Mr. Leery told the kids.

"Over?" Natalie asked. Mr. Leery rushed around his small cottage, gathering his robe and walking stick. Their links waited patiently at the back door.

"It's a wonder no one saw the goblins besides you," Mr. Leery said, then he stopped suddenly and looked at the kids. "No one saw, did they?"

Luke shrugged. "I don't think so. Why?"

"It could cause problems," Mr. Leery responded. "Many, many problems."

"No one else was around," Penny assured him.

Mr. Leery nodded and rubbed his bald head. "Let's go, then."

"Go where?" Natalie asked, stomping her foot.

"Duh," Kirin snorted. "Weren't you listening? He said 'over'. To the other side of magic. To the Shadow Realm."

"Are you nuts?" Luke blurted. "Isn't that where the Queen lives, and all of the boggarts and goblins?"

"Oh, yes," Mo said with a purr. "And trolls and ogres and . . ."

"Hush, Mo," Mr. Leery said.

"Luke's right," Natalie said.

"I am?" Luke squeaked. Natalie had never agreed with him before.

Natalie nodded. "I'm not going anywhere until I've had a long, hot bubble bath."

"No time for that," Mr. Leery said.

Penny grabbed the sleeve of Mr. Leery's jacket. "Wait a minute. Luke has a point. That's where the goblins *came* from. What if there are more waiting for us? Isn't it safer on this side of magic?"

"It won't be," Mr. Leery told her. "The border has been weakening for years. Obviously, the Queen sent those goblins to capture you. Since they failed, I fear the Queen will send something even worse through the gaps in the border."

"Then you need to fix those gaps," Natalie said.

Mr. Leery shook his head. "I have tried my best. But it takes three to keep the border intact. And there haven't been three strong Keyholders in far too long. That's why I need you; but I cannot pass total power to you, because you are not trained. Until then, the Queen, and her henchmen, will be out to get you."

"By henchmen," Mo said, "he means those adorable creatures like the boggarts and goblins and . . ."

"Hush, Mo," Mr. Leery warned. Then he looked at the three kids. "We have no choice but to go over. But do not fear. Where we're going is protected with great magic."

Luke held up his wrist to show his bracelet. "This kind of magic?" he asked.

Mr. Leery shook his head. "Magic much more powerful than that," he said. "Elfin magic." After a quick glance around the neighborhood to make sure no one was looking, Mr. Leery led the procession out his back door to the woods behind his house.

Natalie went, but she complained the whole way. "This has been the worst day of my life," she snapped. "And to think I used to want to hang out with you two." She frowned at Luke and Penny.

Penny looked at Luke in surprise. Did he

know that Natalie had wanted to hang out with them?

Mr. Leery held up his hand. "Pay attention. This is the first, and perhaps your most important lesson. You must open your mind as accepted links to find a magical murmur near the border that separates the land of the humdrums from the land of magic." He waved his hand and a ripple broke through the air. The thorns of the bushes fell away, creating a path into the land of magic.

"How did he do that?" Natalie asked as they all passed through the border and into a clearing. Behind them the thorns clicked and clacked like killer knitting needles, to reform the barrier behind them. "How are we going to get out of here?"

"Don't worry," Luke said. "Mr. Leery can get us out."

"I better write this down," Natalie said. She looked at her hands. She patted her jeans pocket. "Where is it?" she shrieked. "Who stole my notebook?"

Penny and Luke shrugged. They knew the notebook was full of Natalie's rumors. "I hope a goblin ate it for an afternoon snack," Luke muttered.

"Why did you use your walking stick before, if you just need your mind?" Penny asked, trying to get Natalie to think of something else.

Mr. Leery smiled. "I like my stick."

"What about our keys?" Luke said. "I thought Keyholders should get some kind of key."

"Yeah, maybe a nice gold one with a diamond on top," Natalie agreed.

Mr. Leery shook his head. "Oh no, oh no, my dears. You don't *get* a key. You *are* the keys."

"Greetings, Keyholders," an elf called to them. "I've been waiting for you." The old elf stood only as high as Penny's knees and he wore a long waistcoat of faded green velvet. His feet were covered in pointed shoes of a soft, red leather.

Natalie jumped and let out a little squeak when she saw the man who looked like he belonged in a Snow White movie.

"How did you know we'd be here?" Luke asked.

"I felt a disturbance in the border," Bridger told him. "That could only mean one of two things. A break in the border, or a Keyholder. There have been rumors of leaks throughout the day," Bridger added, turning to Mr. Leery. "I have felt something."

"That must have been the three goblins who chased us," Luke said.

Bridger put his hand over his heart in alarm. "Goblins in the humdrums' land?"

"That's right. These three disgusting monkeys tried to drown me with their horrid spit, but I showed them who was boss," Natalie bragged.

"And who," Bridger asked, "is this repulsively

dirty creature who smells like the armpit of a backcountry giant?"

"Excuse me," Natalie snapped. "You'd smell, too, if you'd been forced into a fifty-year-old trash can and rolled down a mountain."

"Pardon me, Bridger. Allow me to make proper introductions," Mr. Leery said. "Children, I would like to introduce you to the Lead Elf of Pleasant Rock, Bridger the Third."

Bridger bowed low to the ground and swept the tiny hat off his bald head.

"Bridger, please allow me to present to you Penny, Luke, and Natalie."

Penny tried a small curtsy when her name was called. Her grandmother had showed her how to do it, and somehow Penny felt it was appropriate, since Bridger was the Lead Elf of Pleasant Rock.

Luke followed Bridger's example and made a bow, but Natalie sniffed and flicked a piece of dried goblin goo off her sleeve.

Bridger looked confused, but Mr. Leery shook his head at Natalie. "Young lady, do not anger a Lead Elf. It would not be wise," he said.

Natalie threw her hands up in the air. "*Excuse* me."

"Tell me about the goblins," Bridger asked. "Did they touch the Keyholders?"

Mo shook his head. "No. The Keyholders wore their protective silver, but the goblins were brazen, waiting for them in ambush."

Dracula, Kirin, and Buttercup, who had been uncharacteristically quiet, moved closer to their links.

Mr. Leery rubbed his bald head. "This is not good. Not good at all," Mr. Leery whispered.

Bridger's eyes flashed at the Keyholders and he put his hat next to his heart. "You are right, Leery. As always. This can only mean one thing: The Queen is prepared to strike!"

7

"Oh dear, oh dear," Mr. Leery said, wringing his hands. "We must hurry."

Dracula bounced up and down. "Hurry! Hurry! Hurry!" he said. Between each word he snorted a blue-tinged puff of smoke. On the fourth bounce he hit a tree limb.

"Ouch," Dracula said when he landed with a thump next to Luke.

Luke rubbed the purple scales on Dracula's head. "Calm down," Luke told him. "You're going to have a headache for a week after that."

Dracula shook his head, leaving curly smoke

tendrils above his nose. "But Leery says to hurry, hurry, hurry. The Queen is going to strike! Let me at her! Let me at her!" The dragon snorted a stream of blue flames at the ground right where Buttercup sat chewing on a piece of tree bark.

"Yikes!" Buttercup leaped onto Kirin's tail just in time. Then the rat scampered up to the unicorn's back. Buttercup didn't stop until she had buried herself in Kirin's mane.

"Everybody hold your horses," Bridger said.

"Hey! I resent that," Kirin said with a stomp of her hoof that shook Buttercup loose. The rat barely caught the end of Kirin's mane in time. Buttercup scrambled back up between Kirin's ears so she could hold on to the unicorn's horn.

Mr. Leery stepped between Bridger and the unicorn. "Nobody is ready to battle anyone," he said. "What I meant to say is that we must begin the lessons. Immediately."

"You're making this Keyholder stuff sound about as much fun as doing a page of math problems," Luke muttered.

Mo twirled around Mr. Leery's ankles. "What did you think being a Keyholder was going to be like? Full of fiery magic and thunderbolts?"

"Well," Penny said. "Sort of."

"Oh no, no, no," Mr. Leery told them. "The goal of a Keyholder is to never use magic unless it's absolutely necessary. Only in emergencies would we need fiery magic."

"Um, excuse me," Natalie said. "I do believe goblin goo *is* an emergency."

Kirin tossed her mane and stomped a foot. "Someone muffle the diva," she said.

Bridger ignored both Natalie and Kirin. "The best kind of magic is the kind no one ever sees."

"Then being a Keyholder sounds boring," Natalie said. "I think I'll just go home."

"Wait!" screeched Buttercup. She clasped tufts of Kirin's mane in her tiny claws. She tugged with every word she said. "You can't go home. You just can't. We need you. *I* need you!"

"Ouch," Kirin said. "Ouch, ouch, ouch, ouch."

"Oh. Sorry," Buttercup said, but she didn't let go.

Everyone looked at Natalie.

"What's it going to be?" Mo asked. "Are you in? Or are you out?"

"Say you'll stay, Natalie," Buttercup begged. "Pleeeeeeeaaase?"

"Oh, all right," Natalie said without looking at the rat.

"Terrific," Kirin said, though she didn't sound like she thought so at all. "Now get this rat off my head."

Natalie sighed and stepped close enough for Buttercup to leap onto her shoulder. Once there, Buttercup grabbed one of Natalie's hair ribbons and started nibbling.

"You had me worried. Really worried," Buttercup mumbled. "Worried, worried, worried."

"Well, I'm still here," Natalie said. "So if we don't get to throw thunderbolts around, what *do* we do?"

Mr. Leery rubbed his hands together. "It's really quite simple," he said. "A Keyholder's primary responsibilities revolve around maintaining a secure border."

"Huh?" blurted Luke.

"What?" asked Penny.

"In English, please?" snapped Natalie. "We haven't got all day, you know."

"You keep the bad guys out and the good guys in," Mo said.

"Well, in a sense," Mr. Leery said. "That's true. A Keyholder searches for breaches in the border."

"We're looking for old-fashioned pants?" Natalie interrupted.

Mo snickered. "Maybe we should just hand

the world of the humdrums over to the Queen right now."

"Hush, Mo," Mr. Leery said. "No, not those kinds of breeches. I'm talking about holes in the border. As Keyholders, you must be able to sense a gash in the border between the world of reality and the world of magic. Once found, the holes must be mended."

"You've got to be kidding," Luke said. "Are you telling me that being a Keyholder is like being a glorified seamstress? You should ask my mother to do the job. She's a killer with a needle and thread."

"No!" Dracula blurted. "No! No! No! I didn't choose your mother! I chose you! You! You! You!"

Everyone darted away from the excited dragon. Everyone but Mr. Leery and Luke.

Luke patted Dracula's nose to stop him from bouncing up and hitting his head again. "I'm sorry, Dracula," Luke said. "I didn't mean it. Really."

Dracula huffed several times, but he finally calmed down.

"Is it safe to come out?" Natalie asked from behind a bush. Her hair ribbons were totally frayed and now Buttercup was chewing on her hair. When Natalie pushed Buttercup off her shoulder, the rat landed in a pile of dried leaves. "Leave the hair alone," Natalie warned.

"It's safe," Mr. Leery said. "I believe we're all ready for the first lesson. And remember, there is much more to being a Keyholder. This is just the beginning. But it's an important beginning. Fixing the leaks means stopping the Queen from sending her henchmen to create havoc in the real world. That is no small task. No small task at all."

Natalie nodded at Mr. Leery. "Let's get this over with. I'm getting the creeps being out here in the middle of nowhere. This place is probably crawling with snakes and rats and other horrible, smelly creatures."

"Natalie!" Penny snapped, nodding toward

Buttercup. "You're going to hurt someone's feelings!"

"Who cares?" Natalie fussed.

"If you'd just be nice to Buttercup, I bet you'd really like her," Luke whispered.

"Nice to a rat!" Natalie shrieked, not even trying to be quiet. "Do you think I'm crazy?"

Mo growled, "This is definitely not going well. Buttercup, why don't you quit the act and just show Natalie? Maybe that will shut her up."

"Show me what?" Natalie asked.

"Nothing," said Buttercup with a sniff. "Get on with the lesson."

Mr. Leery and Bridger put blindfolds on them, twirled them around, and asked them to sense the border.

Natalie was able to find it every time, no problem. "Ha!" she said after correctly finding the border for the fifth time. "Top that!"

Penny and Luke never could find it. Luke ran

into a tree and Penny stumbled over a bush. They both ended up sitting on the ground.

"Losers," Natalie sang out. "Not only can I find the border, but I can tell that this spot here isn't as strong," she said, pointing right in front of her. Since she still had on her blindfold, she couldn't see Buttercup swell with pride.

Penny and Luke peeked under their blindfolds to see where Natalie pointed. To them, the bushes and trees looked the same as the rest of the border.

Mr. Leery stopped the lessons. He closed his eyes and seemed to take a quick nap. But he wasn't sleeping. His eyes flew open.

"The girl is right!" he said. "The border is stretched to the point that it's ready to snap. This must be where the goblins leaked through. Quickly, Mo."

Mo leaped onto Mr. Leery's arm. When the old man cradled the cat, a low hum filled the clearing. At first, Luke thought it was Mo purring, but then he noticed a faint blue tinge surrounding the man and cat.

"They must be creating a force field," Luke said.

He thought he was talking just loud enough for Natalie and Penny to hear, but Bridger heard him. "A field of magic that only two links can create," Bridger told them.

"I'd better write this down," Natalie said. She looked for her notebook, but then remembered that she'd lost it. As soon as she washed her hair and took a very long bubble bath, she was getting a new notebook; maybe a nice purple one that matched the amethyst on her bracelet.

The kids watched as Mo and Mr. Leery sent their magical field over the thorns and leaves of the border. Slowly, the bushes grew thicker until the tangled branches formed a wall as thick and impenetrable as the cement walls of their school. Gradually, the blue field surrounding the man and cat began to fade.

"Thank you, Natalie," Mr. Leery said. His voice was tired and his skin had turned as gray as a moldy old dish towel.

"Do you think something big got through the leak?" Kirin asked. For once, her voice was gentle, barely more than a whisper.

"I hope not," Mr. Leery said. "For all our sakes."

8

Luke and Penny got to school early the next morning. They waited for Natalie behind the Morgantown Elementary School sign. "Who is she talking to?" Luke asked when Natalie finally showed up.

Natalie was alone on the sidewalk, but she was talking as if she were surrounded by a crowd.

"Maybe she has one of those wireless headsets," Penny said.

"She'd better not," Luke said. "They're not allowed in school."

They waited until Natalie was almost to the sign to call out her name. "Why are you hiding?" Natalie asked when she saw them.

"Why *are* we hiding?" Luke asked Penny.

Penny shrugged. "Just seemed like the thing to do when you're being hunted by goblins," she said.

"Who are you talking to, anyway?" Luke asked as he and Penny stepped out from their hiding place to walk with Natalie.

"Buttercup."

"Buttercup?" Luke asked. "Cool!"

"I wish I could reach Kirin from here." Penny said. She closed her eyes and concentrated on talking to her unicorn in her mind, but all she could hear was Natalie giggling. It wasn't a friendly giggle, either. Penny's eyes flew open just in time for her to see Natalie rolling her eyes at her.

"Duh," Natalie said. "The rat's in my pocket."

"Your pocket?" Penny repeated.

"Are you crazy?" Luke asked. "Links aren't allowed to come to school. Mr. Leery said so."

"Buttercup wanted to come, so I let her," Natalie said, as if that's all it took for her to get anything, which probably was true, since Natalie was the most spoiled kid in Morgantown.

"I thought you didn't like rats," Luke said.

"Well, anything can be improved with a little bling," Natalie told Luke and Penny.

Penny and Luke peeked in Natalie's sweatshirt pocket. Buttercup wore lipstick, pink nail polish, and a lace baby-doll dress that matched the purple of her amethyst collar. She even had clip-on, dangly earrings and a tiny, sparkly tiara!

"You have got to be kidding," Luke said.

"Do you like that stuff?" Penny asked Buttercup.

When Buttercup shrugged the earrings swayed. "Actually, I liked the facial the best of

all. The earrings get a little irritating, but if it makes Natalie happy, I'm okay with it."

"I can't believe you brought your link to school," Penny told Natalie.

"I can't believe you went home and did your nails after being attacked by goblins," Luke said. "Aren't there more important things to worry about?"

Natalie held up her hands to inspect the pink, glittery polish. "Like what?"

"Like the Queen of Boggarts trying to ambush us," Penny hissed.

Natalie shrugged. "I fixed the leak in the border," she said as she flipped her blond ponytail over her shoulder. "No thanks to you."

"Be nice, be nice," Buttercup said. She chewed on the edge of Natalie's pocket, her beady eyes glancing up at her link.

"What if someone finds out about Buttercup?" Luke added. "Did you think of that?"

"What difference does it make?" Natalie asked. "A rat is a rat is a rat."

"Hey, what do you guys have over there?" a kid named Alex asked. He was running up the sidewalk, late as usual. He skidded to a stop so fast his backpack lurched up and bopped him on the back of the head.

Alex rubbed his head and peeked over Luke's shoulder. "A rat! Hey, Thomas, come look at this."

Alex totally ignored all the shushing from Penny and Luke. It didn't take long for a crowd of kids to surround them, squealing over the rat. Buttercup hunkered in the pocket, pulling on her whiskers and staring back up at all the faces looking at her.

"I can't believe Natalie has a rat," Alex said.

"Aren't you afraid it'll poop in your pocket?" Thomas asked.

"Sneaking a rat into school is totally cool," someone else said.

"Leave it to Natalie to dress a rat like a princess," somebody else said.

Natalie smiled at the crowd around her.

"That's because I am the Queen of Cool," she said.

"You have to promise to keep this a secret," Penny told the kids.

"Why?" Alex asked.

"Because," Luke said, thinking fast, "it'll be awesome if Natalie can get through the day without being caught. That way it'll be as if we're all in on it."

"It's a deal," Thomas said.

"Our lips are sealed," Alex added.

The kids had to hurry to get to class. Just before they went into their room, Penny pulled Natalie aside. "You are going to be in so much trouble if Buttercup gets caught."

"Caught?" squeaked the rat in Natalie's pocket. "What happens if I get caught? Will I be covered in goblin goo? Smothered in troll spit? Boiled with ogre eggs?"

"If you get caught by Mr. Crandle, it could be even worse," Penny said, though she really couldn't think of anything worse than troll spit and boiled ogre eggs.

Natalie lightly patted her pocket. "Don't worry, Buttercup. My daddy would never let anything bad happen to me." She turned her back on Penny and marched into the classroom.

Everyone was true to their word. No one told Mr. Crandle about the rat in Natalie's pocket, but Penny still didn't feel right. At lunchtime, Penny pulled Luke to the back of the line as the rest of the kids filed out of the classroom. "I feel like someone is watching me," Penny said.

"Me, too," Luke whispered. "It's giving me the creeps."

"I don't see any boggarts," Penny said.

"I don't see any goblins," Luke added. "What could it be?"

Penny glanced around the room again. That's when she saw it. A pure white hoof had slipped out from under the web of invisibility that the giant spider had weaved for them. "Oh no," Penny groaned. "We're in trouble. Big trouble."

She made sure everyone in her class was gone. Then she closed the door. "All right you two. Come out."

The air in the far corner of the room shimmered as if someone was turning a bright flashlight on and off. Then a long horn poked out of nowhere, followed by Kirin's head. Kirin stepped out from behind her invisibility web. Dracula was perched on the unicorn's back.

"It's me, Luke! It's me!" the dragon said. "Did you miss me? Huh? Huh? Did you?"

"Are you crazy?" Luke blurted. "You're not supposed to be here!"

Dracula's wings slumped and his eyes drooped. "You're not happy to see me?"

"Not here!" Luke said. "Not at school!"

"What if you got caught?" Penny asked.

"It's not like we weren't careful," Kirin

snapped. "We slathered Snuffles' web all over us so no humdrum could possibly spot us. You didn't even know we were here."

"We had to come," Dracula said. "Had to! Just had to!"

Luke reached out and rubbed Dracula's snout to calm him. "Why?"

Kirin stomped a foot. "You two are clueless, aren't you?" she asked, but she didn't wait for an answer. "Remember that leak Natalie helped fix? Well, we got to thinking. What if there's another? The Queen could send hundreds of bumbling goblins through a tear before Mr. Leery could fix it."

Penny looked at Luke. Luke looked at Penny. "They have a point. What are we going to do?" he asked.

"Right now, we have to hide our links," Penny said.

"Aren't you forgetting about our web?" Kirin asked.

"No," Penny said. "I'm not forgetting that the web can slip off in a heartbeat. Now follow me."

A few minutes later, Luke and Penny pushed their links into a janitor's closet. Penny worked to straighten Snuffles' web over their links so that they couldn't be detected even if someone opened the door.

Dracula sniffed a mop bucket and turned pale. "Why are we here?" the dragon asked.

"To keep you safe," Luke explained. "Nobody will think to look for you in here."

"But you're the ones who are not safe. Goblins could be anywhere!" Kirin gently touched her horn to Penny's forehead. "Why else would I risk coming here when you said not to?"

"That's right," said Dracula. "We're here to protect you." Then Dracula sneezed and a broom collapsed in ashes.

"We have to get you out of here before

you burn the school down," Penny said, but when she opened the door her teacher was waiting.

Mr. Crandle glared down at the two kids. "And what, exactly, do you think you are doing?"

Luke glanced behind him to make sure the magic spider's web of invisibility was still working. He saw nothing but mops and brooms and the slop sink. "Um. Er. The juice leaked out of my lunchbox and Penny was helping me clean it up," Luke lied.

Kirin nudged a mop into Penny's hands and Penny held it up as proof.

Mr. Crandle looked at the mop before stepping aside. "You kids get to the lunchroom, or you won't have a chance to eat." Then their teacher sniffed and frowned at the broom ashes on the floor. "What's that smell? Is something on fire?"

"Nope," Penny said as she closed the door. "Just cleaning fluids."

Mr. Crandle followed the kids back to the lunchroom and watched them like a hawk for the rest of lunch.

Penny was hoping Kirin and Dracula would stay in the closet, but when she felt something brush by her she knew it was Kirin. Penny tried talking to her link in her head, but she didn't think it worked.

If it had been a typical day, everyone would've noticed something unusual was going on with Luke and Penny. But thanks to Natalie, nobody gave them a second thought. Natalie kept peeking in her pocket and whispering. When Mr. Crandle wasn't looking, she would let Buttercup run across her desk. Natalie would scoop Buttercup back into her pocket and look totally innocent when the rest of the class collapsed into giggles. By the end of the day, Mr. Crandle's lips were clenched in a straight line and he did not look happy at all.

Neither were Luke and Penny. "Dracula is really worried," Luke said. "I think he's going to blow."

"How do you know?" Penny asked.

Luke shrugged. "I just feel it. Like butterflies in my nose. He thinks the goblins are closing in on us. We have to get to Leery."

Penny nodded. She had felt butterflies, too. Only her butterflies were making her snap at her friends.

As soon as the bell rang, Penny and Luke rushed from their room. "Natalie will do anything for attention," Luke huffed as they walked out of the school. He was pretty sure Kirin and Dracula followed them because he heard Dracula's wings fluttering.

Penny and Luke had just reached the Morgantown Elementary sign when Natalie's cries stopped them dead in their tracks. "Help me! Help me! You have to help me!" she cried.

"What's wrong? Won't your father buy you

new hair ribbons?" Luke asked when Natalie had caught up with them.

Two tears rolled down Natalie's cheeks. "This is serious," she said.

"What happened?" Penny asked Natalie before Luke could make fun of her tears.

"It's Mr. Crandle," Natalie said. "He took Buttercup!"

"He what?" Luke gasped.

"Oh, no!" Penny cried. "This is terrible."

More tears dribbled down Natalie's face. "It's all my fault. I made Buttercup show off today. Now she's been ratnapped. What if Mr. Crandle takes her to the dog pound? What if they kill her?"

"Why do you care?" Kirin said from under her invisibility web, "You don't like her anyway."

Natalie shook her head. "You're wrong. I do care."

"But she's a rat. A rat! Rat-rat-rat! You don't like rats," Dracula reminded her.

Natalie held her hands to her ears. "Stop it!"

she shrieked. "Buttercup's not just a rat. She's my *link!*"

"Calm down, calm down," said a tiny voice from the shadows of the sign. "It takes more than a fifth-grade teacher to get rid of a link."

"Buttercup!" Natalie squealed. "You escaped!" She scooped up the rat and snuggled her under her chin.

Natalie hugged her tight until Buttercup squeaked, "A little air, please!"

Luke shook his head. "Natalie hugging a rat. Now, that's something I never thought I'd see."

"It looks as if that link is complete," Penny said.

"Took her long enough," Kirin's voice said from behind the web, but Natalie didn't pay any attention.

Buttercup and Natalie crossed the street with Natalie smoothing the rat's hair down and hugging her. "Come on, Buttercup. Let's go home and fix your nail polish."

As Natalie hurried away, Buttercup scrambled

to her shoulder to look back at Penny and Luke. The rat waved a tiny paw, then she snuggled up under Natalie's chin to ride the rest of the way home in style.

9

Smack! Penny swatted at an ant crawling up her leg. Scratch! She rubbed her other leg. She was supposed to be concentrating, but the long grass in Luke's backyard was tickling her. And her legs hurt from sitting cross-legged so long.

"This is impossible," she said, flopping back on the grass.

Luke sat right beside her with his eyes closed, facing the bushes at the back of his yard. Instead of playing basketball as he did every Saturday, he and Penny were trying to contact Snuffles, the giant spider.

"It's all your link's fault," Luke said. "If Kirin's horn hadn't torn the web we wouldn't have to worry about getting a new one from Snuffles."

"Don't blame Kirin," Penny snapped. "Dracula's the one that ate wild turkberries. He sneezed so much it made the web look like Swiss cheese."

Luke couldn't argue. He knew his best friend was right. He also knew that if they couldn't convince Snuffles to weave a new invisibility web, their links would be exposed for everyone to see. And that, Mr. Leery had warned them, would spell doom for all. "I wish Mr. Leery would just call Snuffles for us," Luke said.

Penny stared up at the clouds floating in the sky. "He could, but he and Mo are too busy looking for stray goblins. Besides, it's good practice for us."

Sweat trickled down Luke's back under his T-shirt. He smelled the open bag of vinegar potato chips beside him and his stomach rumbled.

He was trying to feel the border, but the only thing he felt was mad.

"This is crazy," he finally told Penny, opening his eyes. "I can't sense anything. How come Natalie can feel the border and we can't?"

Penny sighed. It just didn't seem fair that Natalie could do it and they couldn't. After all, she had everything a kid could want. She had expensive toys, huge TVs, and even a swimming pool in her backyard. Why did she have to be a better Keyholder, too?

"Maybe we're just not trying hard enough," Penny suggested. One thing she'd learned in school is that if she kept trying she eventually solved the problem.

"We've been trying for over a week," Luke said. "I've hardly played any basketball and my mom got mad at me for not cleaning my room." He took a big handful of chips and stuffed them in his mouth.

"But we have to find Snuffles," Penny said,

"so she can make another magic web." Penny sighed. Natalie even had an easier time hiding her link. She could put Buttercup in her pocket. Hiding a unicorn and a dragon wasn't so easy.

"Maybe if we could have our links around us more we could get better at this," Penny said, stretching her legs out in front of her and taking a bite of a chip.

Luke groaned and threw himself down on the ground. "Why won't Snuffles come? Then I could play basketball at least."

Who would've guessed that Snuffles would like vinegar potato chips? At least, that's what Mr. Leery had told them would get Snuffles to make a new web for their links, but it wasn't working.

"I think she's mad because Dracula burned up the first web so quickly," Penny said. "You need to keep him away from those dumb turkberries. Every time he sneezes, he burns up something."

"Kirin tore it with her horn," Luke said. "It's just as much her fault."

"This is just not working," Penny told him as tears stung her eyes. "What if Leery is wrong? Maybe we're not the *real* Keyholders. Maybe Natalie is the true Keyholder and someone else is supposed to help her. Mr. Leery should have asked Alex and Thomas." She wasn't sure she had wanted to be a Keyholder in the first place, but now that she couldn't do even the first lesson she felt sad. The thought of losing Kirin was almost more than she could stand.

"Shh," Luke said.

"What's wrong?" Penny asked, wiping the tears from her eyes.

"I don't think we're supposed to talk about stuff like that so close to the border," Luke told her.

"What difference does it make? We haven't heard a thing and we've been sitting here for an hour."

"But Mo said the goblins wouldn't give up," Luke whispered.

"Don't worry," Penny said. "The book I read of Mr. Leery's said that goblins will never hurt children, even if ordered to do so."

"Well, that's a relief," Luke said. "You could have told me that a week ago and I wouldn't have been afraid to take out the trash at night."

"Sorry," Penny said, eating another chip.

"But if goblins don't hurt kids, then why did the Queen of Boggarts send them after us?" Luke asked.

Penny shrugged. "I guess they're just supposed to kidnap us and take us to the Queen."

"Oh," Luke said. "Forget about taking out the trash tonight."

Luke grabbed a handful of chips. Before he stuffed them in his mouth, he asked, "What else did that book say about goblins?"

"Save some of those for Snuffles," Penny said.

Luke crunched the chips and frowned. "I

don't think she's coming. Tell me what the book said."

"Well," Penny said, licking the salt off her fingers. "They don't like horseshoes."

"That's why Mr. Leery hung a horseshoe on his front porch," Luke interrupted.

Penny nodded. "Four-leaf clovers are supposed to protect you from them, too."

Luke rolled over and pawed through the grass around him. Penny leaned over and looked for clovers, too, but she found nothing.

"I guess my dad got rid of all the clover last fall," Luke said after they'd spent several minutes hunting.

"What else?" Luke asked, wiping his hands on his pants.

"What else what?" Penny said, watching a worm in the grass.

"What else don't goblins like?" Luke snapped. All this concentrating on the border was making him more than a little grumpy.

"Let me think," Penny said, looking up in the sky. "Oh yeah, they like to throw things and pinch people."

"Ouch!" Luke teased, acting like a goblin pinched him.

"Very funny," Penny said. "If you throw seeds at them, they have to stop to pick them up. And the book said that a gift of new clothes will send them away forever."

"That's weird," Luke said.

"This whole thing is weird," Penny agreed. "Oh, the book also said that it was unwise to speak of them. One other thing."

"What?" Luke said.

"There are different kinds of goblins. The little dumb ones like the ones we saw, and a bigger, smarter version. They're known as hobgoblins."

When Penny told him that, a strange feeling went through Luke's body. "Penny," he shouted. "You're not going to believe this. I think I felt the border!"

No sooner were the words out of his mouth than the bushes right in front of them crackled and snapped like they were on fire, but there was no fire.

"What's happening?" Penny asked.

Luke gulped. "I don't think this is Snuffles."

Penny grabbed the bag of chips and crushed it to her chest. Both kids leaped off the ground as the border exploded in front of their eyes.

It was not Snuffles. And it wasn't goblins. No. These were much bigger. Much slimier. And they looked much, much meaner.

"Hobgoblins," Penny gasped.

Beasts, taller than Luke's basketball goal and covered with matted orange hair, crashed through the border. There weren't three. Not six. There were fifteen! And these hobgoblins weren't giggling or slobbering or bumping into each other. They looked serious. Very, very serious.

Penny and Luke backed away from the border.

"Do you think those guys have read that part in your book about not hurting kids?" Luke whispered.

Penny tried to talk, but nothing came out of her mouth. All she knew was that they had to warn Mr. Leery. He was the only one who could help them now. He was the only one who could stop the hobgoblins from going crazy in the real world and ruining the secrecy of the border.

The hobgoblins burst from the broken branches onto the tall green grass of Luke's yard. Penny pointed toward Mr. Leery's yard and Luke nodded.

"One, two, three, run!" Luke yelled and the kids dashed for the safety of Mr. Leery's house.

10

They didn't make it to Mr. Leery's. Hob-goblins came from everywhere and surrounded them. "Show them your bracelet," Penny yelled. She pulled her shirt sleeve up, but it wasn't there.

"Oh, no! It must've fallen off at home when I took off my sweatshirt." Penny groaned. "Hurry, show them yours."

A huge hobgoblin with green teeth jumped right in front of them. Luke screamed and Penny kicked the creature in the knee. Penny and Luke dashed around the fallen monster.

"What are you waiting for?" Penny yelled as they ran. "Show them your bracelet."

"I didn't wear it. I didn't think we needed it anymore. Besides, it's too girly. I left it at home." Luke wished more than anything that he'd worn the silly bracelet anyway. He knew if he ever got away from these monsters, he'd wear his bracelet from now on.

Wham!

Wham!

Wham!

Hobgoblins fell from trees all around them. "We're done for," Penny yelled.

"This is the end," Luke said as he covered his eyes to wait for the monsters to squash him like a bug.

He expected to hear growls.

He expected to hear bones crunching.

But that's not what he heard at all.

Ring. Ring. Jingle. Jingle.

The hobgoblins shrieked in agony at the sound.

"What's happening?" Luke asked, looking around to see what was ringing.

Ring. Ring. Jingle. Jingle.

The monsters covered their ears. They shook their heads and cringed. They turned and ran, kicking up big clods of dirt and grass, and pushing their way back to the other side of magic. Torn leaves and splintered branches marked their path.

Two lone figures remained, standing in the cloud of dust.

"Natalie!" Penny gasped.

Natalie had a dozen bells in each hand and she was shaking them like crazy. Buttercup stood on the ground beside her, shaking the large bell in her mouth and the three hanging from her tail.

Even when Luke grabbed the bell out of Buttercup's mouth, her body still shook. "How did you know what to do?" Penny asked.

"Don't you guys pay attention at all?" Natalie said, rolling her eyes. "Boggarts and goblins hate bells."

Penny did something she never imagined doing. She hugged Natalie. "Thank you for saving us."

Natalie pushed Penny away and gave her a strange look.

"But how did you know we were under attack?" Luke asked.

Natalie pointed to her house. "I can see everything from my window. I watch you guys playing all the time."

Bam! Dracula slammed into Luke, knocking him to the ground. "I'm here! I'm here! Are you all right?"

"I was until you knocked me down," Luke told him. Luke stood up and dusted grass off his pants.

Kirin jumped over the bushes between Luke and Mr. Leery's yard and nuzzled Penny. Even Mo slid through the bushes. "I felt that you needed us," Kirin explained.

Penny threw her arms around Kirin. "We did! There were horrible hobgoblins everywhere."

Mo sniffed the air. "Mmmmrrrrruuuccck. Hobgoblins? More than one?"

"Lots more," Luke said.

"This is not good," Mo said. "Not good at all."

"Why is this any worse than the boggarts or the three goblins we saw before?" Penny asked.

Mo blinked his amber eyes. "Because," he said, "hobgoblins are smart. Much smarter than boggarts and goblins. Bigger, too. If hobgoblins can just barge through the barrier, then that means the magic has been nearly destroyed. Which means only one thing. The Queen has learned how to undo the magic that has kept us safe for centuries. Not only that, they chose Luke's backyard. That was no accident. The Queen's forces are getting smarter. They're zeroing in on you. Hunting you like a cat hunts a rat," he said.

"Hey!" squeaked Buttercup. "I resent that."

"Sorry," Mo said, but he didn't sound like he meant it. "Where did the hobgoblins go? Please don't tell me they're rampaging down the street for every humdrum to see."

"Don't worry," Luke told him. "They went back to the other side of magic."

"They didn't just go away," Natalie bragged. "I chased them back with all these bells. If it wasn't for me, Penny and Luke would be goblin soup by now." Natalie clanged the bells in her hands and nodded to Buttercup. "Of course, Buttercup helped."

Kirin nuzzled closer to Penny. "That's it!" Kirin snapped. "I'm not letting you out of my sight ever again."

Penny hugged Kirin's neck. "But it's dangerous for you to be out in the open. What would my parents say if they saw a unicorn with me?"

Kirin tossed her mane. "They would say they have one very lucky daughter."

Penny laughed and Dracula bounced up and down. "Me, too. Me, too. I'm going to be with Luke always."

Luke didn't know what to say. He didn't

want to hurt his link's feelings, but he didn't know how he could explain a dragon to his parents. He glanced toward his house, hoping nobody was looking out the back windows. "Maybe we'd better go tell Mr. Leery about the hobgoblins."

"Wait just a minute," Buttercup told them.

Natalie handed her bells to Penny and giggled. "Just watch this," Natalie said.

Buttercup and Natalie sat in front of the splintered bushes where the beasts had broken through. Buttercup climbed into Natalie's lap and they both stared in silence at the damage. Then they closed their eyes.

"Come on, Natalie," Penny said in an irritated voice. "We don't have time for you to show off how you can find a weak spot. We can all see that it's weak."

Natalie didn't brag, but a noise did fill Luke's yard. It started as a low hum, but then grew into a loud buzz. "What's happening?" Luke asked Kirin. "Are the hobgoblins coming back?" Luke looked all around, clutching the bell in his hand.

"Watch and learn," Kirin said. For once, her voice was filled with awe instead of sarcasm.

Penny gasped as a faint blue glow surrounded Natalie and her rat. The glow grew stronger and deeper. Then without warning, the bushes and branches that the monsters had broken flew back together.

Clack. Click. Clack. Click. Like a giant knitting machine, the thorns on the bushes wove themselves back together. In minutes, the bushes and trees looked like they'd been there for centuries. There wasn't a single broken branch or even a snapped twig.

"How did she do that?" Luke asked, rushing over to look at the bushes.

Natalie opened her eyes and smiled. "And that is how a real Keyholder fixes the border."

Penny frowned. "When did you learn how to do that?"

Natalie stood up and brushed grass off her white jeans. "While you two were still working on lesson one, Mr. Leery showed me lesson two."

"That's not fair!" Luke said. "We're supposed to learn stuff together!"

"Why should I have to wait on you guys?" Natalie asked. "You might never learn how to feel a weakness in the border."

Penny felt a cold pain in her stomach. What if Natalie was right?

"Besides, it's a good thing he showed me," Natalie continued. "Buttercup and I fixed it before anything else could get through."

Dracula hopped up and down. "Good job! Good job!"

Luke was irritated, too. "Be quiet, Dracula. Let's go tell Mr. Leery about the hobgoblins."

Just then, a noise unlike anything they'd ever heard came from Mr. Leery's house.

"Leery!" roared Mo.

11

"He's got to be here!" Penny screamed.

Kirin, Natalie, Buttercup, Luke, Dracula, and Penny checked the yard, but couldn't find a trace of Mr. Leery. Inside his cottage, they searched behind every pile of books, under the bed, behind the doors, and even under the kitchen table.

Mr. Leery was nowhere to be found.

"Maybe he went for a walk," Natalie suggested.

Penny picked his walking stick up off the living room floor. "He left this."

"Mrrrrrrnooooo! He never leaves home without his stick," Mo told them. "Never."

"Does this place have some kind of secret passage or hiding place?" Luke asked. He hoped that maybe Mr. Leery was just hiding. Luke didn't want to think anything bad had happened to his good friend.

Mo was quiet and Penny stared at him. "Is there a secret place?"

Mo licked his hand and ruffled his fur. "I don't think Mr. Leery would want you to know about it yet."

Natalie stuck her finger into Mo's face. "Listen here, you mangy little cat. We're Keyholders, for goodness sake. The time for secrets is over. Show us the secret place."

Luke remembered how Mo could change into a griffin and warned Natalie. "Um, Natalie. I don't think you should talk to Mo that way."

Mo growled, but he turned and went into the

kitchen. He put his paws on a small button on the refrigerator door and it sprang open.

"Watch out," Penny told everyone. "If Mr. Leery didn't throw away his milk, it's going to smell horrible by now."

The last time Penny had opened Mr. Leery's refrigerator, the milk had been spoiled. But this time the kids didn't see milk; they didn't see the inside of a refrigerator at all.

They saw a small room with walls of polished red marble. Thick, red wool rugs were thrown casually on a gleaming cherrywood floor. A big armchair of green velvet sat beside a stone fireplace. Beside the chair, piles of books covered the floor. Massive wooden bookcases held more huge leather tomes with gold letters on the spines. Flickering candles perched in brass holders hung from the walls, casting a soft glow over the elegant room.

"Wow!" Natalie said. "I've got to get a refrigerator like this one."

"How did he do that?" Luke asked Penny. "When you opened it before, it was just a refrigerator."

Penny shook her head. "There must be a special button or something."

Mo darted into the room, followed by Luke, Penny, Natalie, Dracula, Kirin, and Buttercup. It only took a minute for them to see that Mr. Leery was not there.

"Is there another secret place?" Penny asked hopefully.

"Mmmmmrrrrnnnno," Mo said in the most mournful moan the kids had ever heard.

"He's been taken," Kirin said.

Dracula bounced up and down. "Hobgoblins got him. Hobgoblins got him."

"But why?" Luke said.

"Natalie has not had her ceremony yet and you are only apprentices," Mo told them. "You've only begun to learn. Leery is still a powerful Keyholder, the most powerful Keyholder of all."

Buttercup scrambled up onto the pile of books. She pulled her whiskers. "But he still has so much to teach you. How will you learn? How will any of us learn?"

Mo hissed. "Don't worry. Leery and I will teach you after I get back."

"Back? Where are you going?" Luke asked.

"You can't go anywhere," Penny told him. "We need your help."

Mo hissed again and began to grow. His front legs grew raptor's talons and his hind legs changed into a lion's. His whiskers unfurled into a razored beak. Wings sprang from his sides. The hair between his ears changed into a golden crest.

"What's he doing?" Natalie asked. "Is he one of those monsters from the yard? Where are the bells?"

"No," Luke told her. "We don't need the bells. He's a griffin. He can change shapes."

"What in the world is a griffin?" Natalie asked.

"A griffin is a creature with deadly claws," Penny whispered.

Luke looked at her strangely. "How do you know that?"

"My book of enchanted creatures, of course," Penny said proudly, glad to be able to at least know something that Natalie and Luke didn't.

Mo pushed open the refrigerator door with his sharp beak and Natalie grabbed his tail. "Wait, where are you going?"

Mo swirled around. His wings lifted into the air until they touched the ceiling and he opened his beak. Natalie, Penny, and Luke backed away as Mo roared.

Dracula flew beside Luke. Buttercup leaped onto Natalie's sneaker and Kirin stood firmly beside Penny. Penny knew that Kirin was there to protect her if she needed it.

"Mo!" snapped Kirin. "Calm down. We're here to help."

"Yeah," Natalie said. "Don't get your purple feathers all bunched up. I just asked a simple question. Where are you going?"

Mo settled his wings down and glanced around the room like he was looking at it for the last time—like he might never see it again. Then he said softly, "Why, I'm going to find Leery, of course."

Luke looked at Penny. Penny looked at Natalie. All three looked at their links. And then, together, the three Keyholders stepped forward.

"Then we're all going," Luke said.

"Me, too! Me, too!" Dracula said, bouncing so high his head hit the ceiling.

Kirin nuzzled Penny and nodded, touching her shining horn to the ground before Mo. "We are at your service," she said.

Buttercup scampered between Natalie's sneakers. Her whiskers trembled as she looked up at the three Keyholders towering above her.

Natalie nodded at Buttercup. "We're Keyholders," Natalie said, grabbing Luke's and Penny's hands. "There's no turning back now."

Mo roared, "Let's go rescue Leery."

Turn the page for a sneak peak at

KEYHOLDERS #3

INSIDE THE MAGIC

"Is he dead?" Luke whispered.

Natalie pushed Luke aside. "Of course Mo isn't dead. See his sides moving? That means he's still breathing."

"But just barely," Penny said, falling to her knees beside Mo.

When Luke, Penny, and Natalie opened the door to Mr. Leery's house they expected to find Mo waiting impatiently. Instead they found a huge pile of feathers motionless on the floor.

Usually, their neighbor's link took the form of

a big spotted cat. But when he discovered Mr. Leery had been kidnapped by the Queen of the Boggarts, Mo had turned into his natural form of a griffin.

"Be careful, Penny," Luke warned his best friend.

Penny smoothed the crest of feathers on Mo's head. He looked nothing like a cat anymore. For one thing, he was a lot bigger. Not only that, he had a wicked beak, talons, and powerful wings.

Just a few weeks earlier, Natalie, Luke, and Penny had been three normal kids living in Morgantown. In that short time they had found out that the thick tangle of hedges at the edge of their town was actually a border between the world that they knew and a land of magic, and that they had been chosen by a wizard as apprentice Keyholders.

As Keyholders, the kids were chosen to maintain the border and keep the magic world from leaking into the real world. Part of being a Keyholder was wonderful; for example, having a link—an unbreakable lifelong bond with a magical creature. Mo had been Mr. Leery's link for nearly two hundred years. Kirin, a dazzling young unicorn, had selected Penny. Dracula, a rambunctious dragon about the size of a Doberman pinscher, picked Luke. Natalie, on the other hand, wasn't thrilled that she had been chosen by a rat named Buttercup.

Now Penny found herself cradling the head of a beast with talons that could rip a T. rex in half. It was a lot for a fifth grader to handle.

Mo closed his eyes as a spasm shot through his body. Blue, red, green, and orange feathers drifted to the floor. When he opened his eyes again, they were dull and cold. "The Boggart Queen cast a spell. A spell even more powerful than Leery," he whispered.

Humans and their links from the magical realm were so closely connected that when something happened to one, it affected the other. Judging from the way Mo was suffering, whatever had happened to Mr. Leery was bad. Very bad.

"This is your fault," Luke told Natalie. "If you hadn't taken so long packing your stupid pink suitcases we would've been here to help Mo."

"It is not my fault," Natalie said, glaring at Penny. "She wanted to pack, too."

Penny felt guilty. "Natalie's right," Penny said. "I took too long trying to decide what I might need in the magic land." She looked up at her link. Kirin had once used her unicorn horn to help Penny when she had been hurt rolling down a hill in a garbage can. "Can you help Mo?" she pleaded.

Kirin swished her tail back and forth. "Of course I can," she snapped.

"Wait!" Buttercup squealed, but Kirin kneeled before the fallen griffin and touched her horn to the place right above Mo's heart.

Mo shuddered as if cold water gushed through his veins. A green spark exploded from the spot where Kirin's horn touched the griffin's feathers.

"Ouch!" screamed the unicorn. She fell to the floor as if she'd been struck by lightning.

"What happened?" Penny shrieked.

Dracula bounced across Mr. Leery's living room. "Fire! Fire! Fire!" the small dragon shrieked, sending little flames of his own shooting through the air.

"Stop it! Everyone!" shouted a little, yet very powerful voice. Buttercup was usually a meek rat, but she stomped a back paw in frustration. "The spell on Leery was powerfully cast with a protective shield. Not even unicorn magic can break it."

Kirin struggled up in a clatter of hooves. Her eyes crossed and she snorted when she saw her beautiful horn charred and covered with ash. "My horn! What has that evil queen done to my horn?"

"Your horn will heal itself," Buttercup said. "We have other things to worry about."

Kirin swished her tail so hard she slapped

Natalie on the behind. "What is more important than my horn?" the unicorn snapped.

"Leery is," Buttercup pointed out. "And Mo."

Mo lifted his head and whimpered. He had to force out every word. "Find Bridger. He will know. He can help."

The kids stared in horror as Mo's bones popped and cracked. His body turned in on itself as black hair pushed the feathers from his skin. His beak curled inward until it became the face of a cat. In less than a minute, the griffin was gone and a black spotted cat with curled ears lay before them.

"Mo?" Penny asked. "Can you hear us?"

"He *has* to be able to hear us," Luke said. "We can't find Leery without his help."

But Mo didn't answer them. His breathing was shallow and his paws twitched as if he were locked inside a very bad dream.

"We should call the police," Penny said.

"No!" Kirin told her. "No one can know about the Shadow Realm. No one."

"Besides," Buttercup added, "the police would never believe you."

"Maybe a doctor can help Mo," Luke suggested.

Dracula nudged Luke. "No doctor knows boggart spells."

"The Boggart Queen must be stopped," Natalie said. "And I'm just the one to do it."

"A-hem," came a little voice from the floor.

Natalie looked at her link. "With Buttercup's help, of course."

Dracula hopped up and down. "Stop the Queen! Stop her! Stop her!"

Penny clenched her jaw. Before being kidnapped, Mr. Leery had been training them to find and fix leaks in the border. Natalie was a natural at it. Not Penny and Luke. It rubbed Penny's nerves raw that Natalie could do something better than she could.

"Stop bragging," Luke told Natalie. "Just because you're better at finding leaks in the border, it doesn't mean you're ready to fight the Boggart Queen."

Natalie tapped Luke on the nose with a finger. "I'm more ready than you are."

"Stop it!" Penny said, shoving Natalie and Luke apart. "We need to take care of Mo. Then we'll figure out what to do next."

Luke nodded. "I'll get a pillow and blanket."

"Fine," Natalie said. "I'll get some water."

Kirin blew warm air over the cat, but she was careful not to touch his body. Dracula cried a purple tear when Penny and Luke gently placed Mo on a pillow and covered him up to his chin with a blanket. The cat's whiskers twitched and Mo groaned.

"Where is Natalie with that water?" Penny asked.

"I'll check," Luke said.

After a few minutes, Luke came back to the room waving a piece of paper in the air. "She's gone," he said. "All she left was this note."

Penny looked at Natalie's scrawled words. "'Gone to save the world!'" Penny read out loud. "Is she nuts? We have to catch up to her! She can't do it alone."

"We should let her try," Luke said. "It would serve her right to fail."

Penny grabbed Luke's arm. "But if she fails, she could die. We can't let that happen. Even if it is Natalie."

Luke sighed. "You're right. We'd better hurry."

Luke glanced around the room once more before leaving. He noticed Mr. Leery's walking stick propped in the corner. Luke reached for it, the carved wood feeling solid and fitting his palm perfectly.

"Why are you taking that?" Penny asked.

Luke gripped the stick firmly in his hand. "Because," he said, "I have a feeling Mr. Leery will need it on the way back."

"If we make it that far," Penny said.

About the Authors

MARCIA THORNTON JONES enjoys reading more than anything else. As a teacher, her favorite part of the school day was sharing books with her students. It was that love of reading that drew her to writing. She wanted to write the same kinds of stories that she and her students enjoyed reading. One afternoon she mentioned to the school librarian that she'd always had an interest in writing. The librarian, Debbie Dadey, shared a desire to write stories that would encourage reading skills while promoting a true joy of reading. The next afternoon, Marcia and Debbie met while their students were at lunch and began writing. That story, "Vampires Don't Wear Polka Dots," became the first book in their bestselling series The Adventures of the Bailey School Kids.

Marcia lives in Lexington, Kentucky, with her husband, Stephen, and their two cats. For more information about Marcia, her books, author visits and for activities related to her books, check out Marcia's web site: **www.marciatjones.com.**

Dᴇʙʙɪᴇ ᴅᴀᴅᴇʏ taught first grade before becoming a librarian. It was while teaching that she first realized how much she wanted to write a book for reluctant readers. Her first book, coauthored with fellow teacher Marcia Thornton Jones, was about a mysterious teacher. Since then, Debbie and Marcia have collaborated on more than 125 books with sales of over forty million copies.

Debbie lives in Bucks County, Pennsylvania, with her husband, Eric, three dogs, and three children. Her Web site is **www.debbiedadey .com.**